When I grow up, what shall I be?

Of all the many, many jobs,

I C
AN

BY JERRY S

BE
IG!

MY LIAO

Balfron 01360 440407
Callander 01877 331544
Cowie 01786 816269
Dunblane 01786 823125
Plean 01786 816319

Bannockburn 01786 812286
Cambusbarron 01786 473873
Doune 01786 841732
Fallin 01786 812492
St Ninians 01786 432383
Library HQ 01786 432383

Bridge of Allan 01786 812286
Central 01786 432107
Drymen 01360 660751
Killin 01567 820571

http://www.lib.stirling.gov.uk
STIRLING COUNCIL LIBRARIES

L B

, BROWN AND COMPANY
New York   Boston

Little, Brown and Company

Hachette Book Group
237 Park Avenue, New York, NY 10017
Visit our website at www.lb-kids.com

Little, Brown and Copmany is a division of Hachette Book Group, Inc.
The Little, Brown name and logo are trademarks of Hachette Book Group, Inc.

First International Edition: June 2010

Library of Congress Cataloging-in-Publication Data

Spinelli, Jerry.
  I can be anything! / Jerry Spinelli; illustrated by Jimmy Liao. — 1st ed.
      p. cm.
  Summary: A little boy ponders the many possible jobs in his future, from paper-
plane folder and puppy-dog holder to mixing-bowl licker and tin-can kicker.
  ISBN 978-0-316-16226-5 (HC) ISBN: 978-0-316-10244-5 (INT'L)
  [1. Stories in rhyme.] I. Jimi, ill. II. Title.
  PZ8.3.S7592Iag 2010
  [E] — dc22   2008049177

10 9 8 7 6 5 4 3 2

TWP

Printed in Singapore

The illustrations for this book were done in watercolor and acrylic on watercolor paper.
The text was set in ITC Clearface, and the display type is ITC Franklin Gothic.

which one will be the best for me?

pumpkin grower

dandelion blower

apple
chomper

mixing-
bowl licker

tin-can
kicker

barefooted hopper

snowball smother

gift unwrapper

deep-hole digger

lemonade swigger

honeysuckle smeller

silly-joke teller

best-part saver

good-bye waver

EVERY

So many jobs!

They're all such fun—

I'm going to choose...

ONE!